FRED & ANTHONY

DISCARD

Meet

THE HEINIE GOBLINS FROM THE BLACK LAGOON

By ESILE AREVAMIRP
With ELISE PRIMAVERA

Hyperion Paperbacks for Children/New York

First Edition
1 3 5 7 9 10 8 6 4 2

Printed in the United States of America
ISBN-10: 0-7868-3682-2
ISBN-13: 978-0-7868-3682-6
Library of Congress Cataloging-in-Publication Data on file.
Visit www.hyperionbooksforchildren.com

RAINDROPS KEEP FALLING ON MY HEAD
Words by Hal David; Music by Burt Bacharach
© 1969 (Renewed 1997) NEW HIDDEN VALLEY MUSIC,
CASA DAVID and WB MUSIC CORP.
All Rights Reserved. Used by Permission of ALFRED PUBLISHING CO., INC.

RAINDROPS KEEP FALLIN' ON MY HEAD
From BUTCH CASSIDY AND THE SUNDANCE KID
Lyrics by Hal David; Music by Burt Bacharach
Copyright © 1969 (Renewed) Casa David, New Hidden Valley Music and WB Music Corp.
International Copyright Secured. All Rights Reserved.

FOR THOSE WHO STILL HAVEN'T BOUGHT ANY OF FRED AND ANTHONY'S BOOKS, I HAVE THREE WORDS FOR YOU: <u>COUGH</u> <u>IT</u> <u>UP</u>. IN THE MEANTIME, A SUMMARY IS PROVIDED ON THE FOLLOWING PAGES SO THAT YOU MAY BETTER ENJOY YOUR FIRST FRED AND ANTHONY EXPERIENCE.

FRED & ANTHONY ESCAPE FROM THE NETHERWORLD, ONLY TO MEET THE DEMENTED SUPER-DEGERM-O ZOMBIE

FRED AND ANTHONY WERE POSSIBLY THE LAZIEST TWO KIDS ON THE PLANET EARTH.

WE TOTALLY ADMIT IT.

YUP.

THEY WERE ALWAYS LOOKING FOR WAYS TO MAKE SOME DOUGH TO PAY SOMEONE ELSE TO DO THEIR WORK FOR THEM.

COLD CASH

$

TO AVOID DOING THE HORRIBLE, HIDEOUS HISTORY PROJECT, THEY DECIDED TO WRITE A CHILDREN'S BOOK.

THAT'S WHERE THE REAL MONEY IS.

HARRY POTTER

CHA-CHING!

BUT IT WAS WAY TOO MUCH WORK.

ACTUALLY, THEY NEVER GOT PAST THE TITLE.

SO FRED AND ANTHONY DECIDED TO HELP OLD PEOPLE WITH STUFF.

FLUFF YOUR PILLOW?

TIE YOUR SHOES?

WHICH IS HOW THEY ENDED UP ON THE OUTSKIRTS OF TOWN IN A REALLY OLD, OLD PERSON'S HOUSE.

HOUSE of the GOOEY DEATH

THE STORY ENDS HAPPILY.

BUT THEY NEVER DID DO THE HORRIBLE, HIDEOUS HISTORY PROJECT.

FRED AND ANTHONY **FAILED** HISTORY.

LOSERS!

AS PUNISHMENT, ALL THEIR PEZ AND CHEX MIX WAS LOCKED AWAY HERE.

NO ONE LIKED THEM ANYMORE, EITHER.

NOT A BIG DEAL.

NO ONE REALLY LIKED US ALL THAT MUCH TO BEGIN WITH.

NONETHELESS, TO REDEEM THEMSELVES, THE BOYS DECIDED TO HUNT DOWN THE OCSD ZOMBIE (OBSESSIVE-COMPULSIVE SUPER-DEGERM-O ZOMBIE)...

Fred and Anthony were going to eat Pez and Chex Mix until they were ready to throw up, and watch horror movies until their brains fell out of their heads. It was going to be the perfect summer.

AH, THIS IS THE LIFE!

Fred's grandmother decided that this summer Fred needed to get out of the basement and into the fresh air. Fred needed to be in a place where he could frolic beneath a blue, cloudless sky—a place where he could discover the wonder and beauty in nature—a place where he could make new friends that would last a lifetime. And what place was that?

THE NEXT DAY Fred and Anthony waited outside for the bus to take them to camp, and already they were homesick for Fred's basement. The thought of all those hundreds of hours of horror movies with all those ghosts, monsters, blood, and guts going to waste was really depressing.

REMEMBER THE WAY THE DINGY CINDER BLOCK WALLS WERE SET OFF SO PERFECTLY BY THE FOOD-STAINED LA-Z-BOY CHAIRS?

I LOVED IT THERE SO MUCH.

But a moment later, the boys' spirits lifted when a shiny new bus pulled up.

Inside the bus, *Screaming Meemies* was coming on the TV. There was a refrigerator filled with stuff to drink, and a camp counselor named Krystal.

Unfortunately, as soon as Fred's grandmother was out of sight, the bus came to a screeching halt.

The boys immediately became suspicious.

GUIDE to the NETHERWORLD

Planning a trip to the Netherworld but don't know what to do with the kids?

WHATEVER YOU DO, DON'T SEND THEM TO CAMP PLENTY WAMPUM

It wasn't long before Fred and Anthony figured out what was really going on.

It was just like in the movie *Berserk Grease Monkey Man*, where the yuppie investment bankers wind up at a gas station that has been cleverly disguised as a day spa with the cunning use of bamboo screens. The Berserk Grease Monkey Man takes all the yuppie investment bankers' money, and instead of bathing in exotic spring waters and getting hot stone massages, they are forced to drink large quantities of Dr Pepper and change the oil in Ford Fiestas for all eternity.

CAMP PLENTY WAMPUM MY FOOT— GRANDMA'S BEEN CONNED!

I KNOW! THESE DUDES MUST BE RAKING IN THE DOUGH WITH THIS SCAM! WHY DIDN'T WE THINK OF THIS?

After a dinner of frozen Hot Pockets and warm water, Fred and Anthony were crammed inside a log cabin with twenty-five other campers. They lay awake in their bedbug-infested bunks, but the boys remained positive.

LET'S LOOK ON THE BRIGHT SIDE.

YES, IN THE LIGHT OF DAY I'M SURE THIS WILL ALL BE MUCH BETTER!

Obviously, the twelve-hour bus ride, followed
by the crummy dinner, along with the shock of
being without their Pez or Chex Mix, had
scrambled the boys' brains and put them in an
extreme state of denial.

In the morning, after the ambulance took away two kids with ptomaine poisoning, Fred and Anthony, along with all the other campers, were herded out into a driving rain to participate in the only activity there was at Camp Plenty Wampum: paddling around in leaky canoes on Lake Gitchie Lagoonie all day.

Eight hours later, when they were allowed to come in, Fred and Anthony looked forward to warming up by a campfire.

I CAN'T WAIT FOR THE TOASTED MARSHMALLOWS AND NIGHTLY SING-ALONG AROUND THE CAMPFIRE.

Up until now the boys had tried to remain positive, but there was no longer any denying the gravity of the situation they found themselves in.

ANTHONY, BUDDY—FACE IT— THERE'S NOT *GOING* TO BE ANY SING-ALONG OR CAMPFIRE.

Sure enough, in place of a campfire was a cold pile of sticks; there were no signs of any marshmallows; and instead of a sing-along, they had story time.

. . . SO DEY FILLED DIS GUY'S SHOES WID CEMENT AND TREW HIM IN DA RIVER. DA END.

WHAT KIND OF A STORY IS THAT?

AND WHERE ARE ALL THE MARSHMALLOWS?

THE 1 BURNT MARSHMALLOW MUMMY

Fred and Anthony and all the other campers sat shivering around the cold pile of sticks while the counselors told a strange story. It was a story about obsession, about staring into the abyss of the dark night of the soul. But mostly it was a story about a boy—a boy who ate so many toasted marshmallows that his insides turned into a sort of jamlike substance and he died and became a mummy. But his obsession with toasted marshmallows lived!! Nothing could kill it!!!

To this day, the Burnt Marshmallow Mummy wanders the woods of Camp Plenty Wampum, searching, searching, searching, for toasted marshmallows and for other campers whom he can make into Burnt Marshmallow Mummies like him.

THAT'S HORRIBLE!

IT MAKES ME WANT TO GET IN BED AND COVER UP WITH A WHOLE BUNCH OF SHEETS!

For the second time that night, Fred and Anthony listened to a strange tale—a tale about sheets—short sheets—and the boy who was tormented night after night by finding his bed in this condition.

Eventually the boy was driven completely mad and died. Now his ghost wanders the woods of Camp Plenty Wampum, short-sheeting the beds of campers in the hopes that they, too, will be driven mad and will have to wander the woods for all eternity just like him—the Lone Short-Sheeting Stranger!

41

OR COULD IT?

Eventually the Hot Pockets ran out, and Fred and Anthony were given hardly any breakfast at all.

Then, as usual, they were sent out onto Lake Gitchie Lagoonie in their canoe.

It didn't seem possible that two boys living only on Hot Pockets and dirt would have the strength to outpaddle the Creature from the Black Lagoon.

BUT THEY DID . . .

Everyone was elated to see Fred and Anthony, having thought the boys had met some terrible fate out in the treacherous waters of Lake Gitchie Lagoonie.

Touched by the outpouring of emotion, Fred and Anthony vowed to do anything they could to help their fellow campers get through their days there at Camp Plenty Wampum.

And while they were at it, why not make some wampum of their own?

BUT HOW?

BY GIVING TOURS TO THE NETHERWORLD AND CHARGING ADMISSION

MY BEST IDEA YET!

Fred and Anthony had made up their minds. They would never give up on their dream, and no one could ever stop them! Not Carmine and Vinnie, or the Creature from the Black Lagoon, or the Burnt Marshmallow Mummy, or even the Lone Short-Sheeting Stranger, because it was not only Fred and Anthony's dream but the American dream, and that's what makes this country what it is!

No matter what it took—even if it killed them—they would finally make a ton of dough to pay others to do their work for them!

THE HEINIE GOBLIN

7

FROM THE

BLACK LAGOON

GUIDE to the NETHERWORLD
TIP #8
HEINIE GOBLINS

Seen only when the moon is full, Heinie Goblins are cute little bat-like creatures with purple feathers and bare heinies. They are talkative and outwardly friendly; they like to be the center of attention and are eager to give advice. But beware: it is usually self-serving, and following the advice of a Heinie Goblin will in all likelihood end badly. At the very least, Heinie Goblins are a major pain in the butt.

OH, LOOK, ISN'T HE CUTE?

ADORABLE.

LET'S PARTY LIKE IT'S 1999!

WARNING!!
BORING PART WHERE EVERYTHING GOES RIGHT
For the next few pages nobody gets eaten, mangled, strangled, or sanitized. Worse, Fred and Anthony for the first time will actually make money. We understand that there is nothing more boring or irritating than seeing someone besides ourselves raking in the dough. We do apologize, and please know that it IS crucial to the story and will not last long!

It was a beautiful night in the Netherworld, with a full moon. Fog clung to the green, slime-covered ground, and permeating the air was a strange odor that was a cross between the gym shorts you left in your locker all year long and the banana you left in your locker all year long.

Fred and Anthony's campers met Frankenstein, they visited with some skeletons, and they saw graveyards with hands coming out of graves dripping blood.

At the end of the night everyone met at the Porta Potti by the Black Lagoon to climb back up to camp. The campers agreed it was everything they'd hoped it would be and a good time was had by all.

Fred and Anthony led the campers out of the Netherworld without mishap and later they were amazed to find that for the first time in their lives they were actually making money.

Yes, it looked as though it wouldn't be such a bad summer after all for Fred and Anthony. The boys went to sleep that night tired but happy, and secure in the knowledge that they would soon be rolling in dough.

END OF BORING PART WHERE EVERYTHING GOES RIGHT

8

FRED & ANTHONY SNATCH *failure* from the JAWS of SUCCESS

Fred and Anthony knew they were in for a lot of trouble. It was just like the movie *Island of the Green Toxic Garden Gnomes*, where the hipster collector of medical abnormalities takes a wrong turn on his Ski-Doo and gets trapped on an island that has been completely taken over by green toxic garden gnomes, who are multiplying at an alarming rate.

Fred and Anthony had to act fast!

Upon leaving the Netherworld, it is highly recommended
that one check for the presence of Netherworld pests
in the garments, especially pant cuffs and socks, of all
the gullible people in your party who will believe every
single sob story they hear.

In case of infestation, call

NETHERWORLD EXTERMINATORS PLUS

Residential & Commercial

"We take care of all your extermination needs!"

Specializing in:
*Potty Trolls
*Pantie Ants
*Heinie Goblins

Over 2,000 Years' Experience!
24-HOUR SERVICE
member Netherworld Pest Control
Call: 000-000-0000

In well over their heads, the boys wasted no time and called in the professionals.

But evidently cash flow in the Netherworld wasn't so hot either, because the professionals turned out to be the Lone Short-Sheeting Stranger and the Burnt Marshmallow Mummy, who were moonlighting as exterminators.

It only goes to show that the cycle of abuse is never broken. Yes, dear reader, today's innocent camper whose bed is repeatedly short-sheeted will become tomorrow's Lone Short-Sheeting Stranger. Today's unsuspecting marshmallow toaster can so quickly spiral out of control into tomorrow's Burnt Marshmallow Mummy.

Carmine and Vinnie were two kids with bad camp experiences, and now they were going to exact their revenge!

And while they had no intentions of destroying the world, Carmine and Vinnie—or rather the Lone Short-Sheeting Stranger and the Burnt Marshmallow Mummy—had decided to make all the campers sit around a cold pile of sticks and sing "Kumbaya" until they turned forty.

DA FIRST KID WHO STOPS SINGIN' GETS FED TO DA CREATURE FROM DA BLACK LAGOON. CAPISCE?

HELLO?

WE'RE HERE.

REVENGE OF THE 9 HEINIE GOBLINS

Miraculously, Fred's and Anthony's as well as all the campers' lives were temporarily saved when the Heinie Goblins interrupted the story to complain that they were very unhappy with the lack of attention they had received so far in this book.

IT'S SUPPOSED TO BE **THE HEINIE GOBLINS FROM THE BLACK LAGOON**—REMEMBER?

Fred and Anthony tried to explain that the Lone Short-Sheeting Stranger and the Burnt Marshmallow Mummy had contributed to the story by being greedy, vile, and sadistic, and that all the Heinie Goblins ever did was come up with one stupid idea after another.

OH, YEAH?

YEAH.

Three very important lessons can be taken from what happened next. The first is that seeking revenge is never the answer for dealing with the disappointments in our lives. The Burnt Marshmallow Mummy and the Lone Short-Sheeting Stranger learned this a little too late when a swarm of Heinie Goblins attacked and fed them to the Creature from the Black Lagoon.

YAY!

YAY!

CHOMP!
CHOMP!
YAY!

It had been a horrible, hideous summer indeed—and now this. On the bright side, the Burnt Marshmallow Mummy, the Lone Short-Sheeting Stranger, and all the Heinie Goblins had been eaten by the Creature from the Black Lagoon. On the not so bright side, so had Fred and Anthony.

I THINK I'M STARTING TO SEE THE WHITE LIGHT! GOOD-BYE, OLD FRIEND!

GOOD-BYE—AND JUST IN CASE I MANAGE TO GET OUT OF THIS ALIVE, CAN I HAVE YOUR BASEMENT?

The boys' lives were hanging by a thread—or, rather, by a tooth. Now it was only a matter of time before they would end up falling down into the belly of the Creature, never to be heard from again!

BUT . . . THAT DIDN'T HAPPEN.

The Creature had an appointment with the dentist, and when he opened his mouth, the boys took that lucky opportunity to flee.

Fred and Anthony were once again in a room with a single chair, some drills, and a sink the size of a Frisbee to spit into. It looked just like the room from the first book that they landed in—and if you didn't read it, you have only yourself to blame for not knowing what is going on in this story.

The evil dentist, Dr. Frankenstein III, D.D.S., picked up both boys with the superhuman strength that comes only from years of picking up boys and stuffing them into his Boy-Brain-Extracticator-World-Destroyalator Machine. Yes, it was finally all over for Fred and Anthony!

Fred and Anthony had cheated death but were being killed by the Angry Anonymous Amazon One-Star Reptile People's reviews.

Thankfully, there was someone on Fred and Anthony's side—but who?

When the Angry Anonymous Amazon One-Star Reptile People heard the title for *this* book, they were stirred into even more of a furious frenzy. There was no reasoning with them, even though Fred tried to explain how the title would drive sales through the roof because of how big heinies were in the country right now. And if you don't think that's funny, we suggest you lay off the Chex Mix for a while.

QUICK! CLIMB ON MY BACK, AND I WILL FLY YOU AWAY TO SAFETY!

THAT'S GREAT—BUT IF IT'S ALL THE SAME TO YOU, I'D RATHER NOT CLIMB ON YOUR BACK.

In the nick of time the Heinie Goblins swooped down and helped the boys escape the evil Dr. Frankenstein, the revolting reptilian reviewers, and the creepy Creature from the Black Lagoon.

WE THOUGHT YOU WERE EATEN BY THE CREATURE FROM THE BLACK LAGOON.

WE WERE!

SO WHAT ARE YOU DOING HERE?

As it turned out, Heinie Goblins will do any-thing—even come back from the dead—for a lit-tle publicity. Fred and Anthony thanked them for saving their lives and promised again that their new book would be titled *The Heinie Goblins from the Black Lagoon.*

GREAT!

SO NOW, WHY DON'T WE HIT OURSELVES IN THE HEAD WITH ROCKS AND SEE WHO PASSES OUT FIRST?

NO.

OH, COME ON! YOU GUYS NEVER WANT TO HAVE ANY FUN.

WE HAVE TO BE GOING NOW.

BYE-BYE!

116

THE PERFECT END TO A HORRIBLE, HIDEOUS SUMMER

13

Fred and Anthony found their way back to the loving arms of their families, and what a joyous reunion it was.

YOU'RE HOME EARLY.

THEY WERE FEEDING US DIRT.

WHEN I WAS YOUR AGE, WE WERE LUCKY IF THERE EVEN WAS DIRT.

The boys told their harrowing story of everything that had happened at Camp Plenty Wampum. But in the end, Fred and Anthony chose to see it as a positive experience.

Yes! Coming through all the trials and tribulations of their days at camp had made the boys stronger. The oozing sores all over their bodies from the bedbugs and the scurvy from the malnutrition were but a small price to pay for all that they had gained.

They had learned self-reliance, self-control, and self-empowerment, but most importantly, they learned that in the future they would stay away from Porta Potties and public restrooms in general—not to mention summer camp.

What a summer it had been for Fred and Anthony! They had been short-sheeted, marsh-mallowed, almost eaten by the Creature from the Black Lagoon, reviewed by Angry Anonymous Amazon One-Star Reptile People; they had escaped an evil character from the first book, and been saved by celebrity-seeking Heinie Goblins. The summer had gone by so quickly, as it always does—but it wasn't quite over yet.

Fred's grandmother and Anthony's parents felt terrible about sending them to such a crummy camp, and they wanted to make it up to the boys.

Fred and Anthony were showered with Pez and Chex Mix.

In, fact there was enough Pez and Chex Mix to last for every single show of Celine Dion.

That way, Fred's grandmother and Anthony's parents figured that the boys would be nice and rested . . .

. . . to go back to school.

Now, that's scary!

[9]